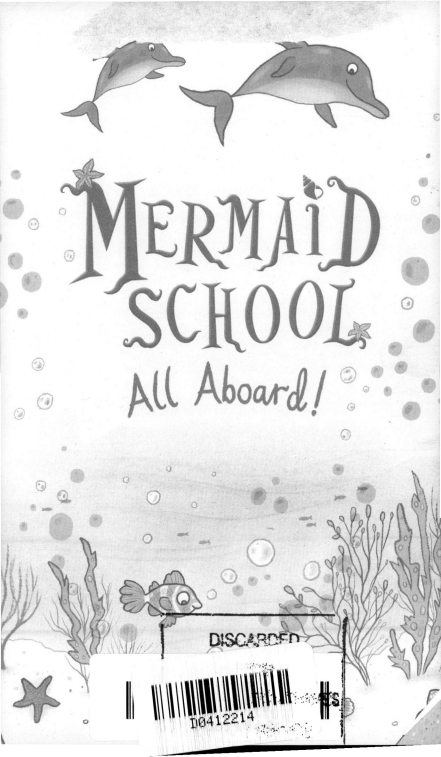

MERMAID SCHOOL

All Aboard!

The Mermaid School series

Mermaid School
The Clamshell Show
Ready, Steady, Swim!
All Aboard!
Save our Seas!

Look out for more in the series!
mermaidschoolbooks.co.uk

MERMAID SCHOOL

All Aboard!

LUCY COURTENAY
ILLUSTRATED BY SHEENA DEMPSEY

Ⓐ
ANDERSEN
PRESS

First published in 2021 by
Andersen Press Limited
20 Vauxhall Bridge Road
London SW1V 2SA
www.andersenpress.co.uk

2 4 6 8 10 9 7 5 3 1

British Library Cataloguing in Publication Data available.

ISBN 978 1 78344 989 7

Printed and bound in Great Britain
by Clays Ltd, Elcograf S.p.A.

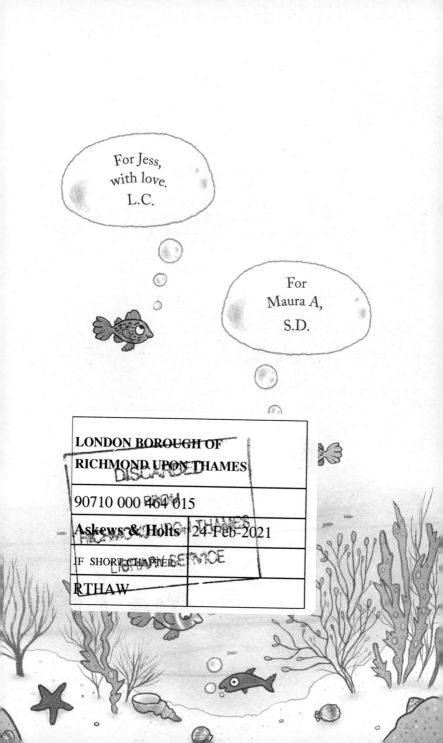

For Jess,
with love.
L.C.

For
Maura A,
S.D.

Chapter One

Marnie Blue stared at her plate.

'Mum?' she said cautiously. 'What *is* it?'

Daphne Blue wiped a blob of green gravy off the end of her nose. 'Algae curry,' she said. 'It's *full* of vitamins.'

Marnie prodded the dark green stew with her driftwood fork. The fork snapped in half. 'It's full of sand too,' she said.

'The sand will help you to digest the curry,' explained Daphne. She sat down at the table in the middle of their little mermaid cave. 'I was reading all about it in the recipe section of *Fishtales Monthly*. We should all have more sand in our diets.'

Marnie put down her broken fork. 'I think I'll wait for Aunt Christabel,' she said. 'Where is she anyway?'

'I have no idea,' Daphne admitted. 'You know what your aunt is like with her galas and fashion launches and music awards. She'll turn up. Eat up before it goes cold!'

'It's already cold,' Marnie pointed out, a little gloomily.

'Well, eat up anyway,' said Daphne. 'We have a big day tomorrow and we are going to need all the energy we can get!'

Marnie cheered up a bit. The first years at Lady Sealia Foam's Mermaid School were going on a school trip to Queen Maretta's Palace. Her mum had filled in all the forms, and paid for Marnie's ticket. She had even volunteered to come along and help. Marnie was looking forward to it more than anything. She hoped she'd be in a group with her two best friends, Pearl Cockle and Orla Finnegan.

She looked out of the window at Mermaid Lagoon. There was no sign of Christabel's blue sea-moss coat, or her aunt's cheeky little goldfish Garbo on her crystal-studded lead. It was very unlike her glamorous radio-star aunt to be late for dinner. Maybe Christabel was visiting her human boyfriend, Arthur.

Christabel was in a LOT of trouble about Arthur. Humans weren't allowed in Mermaid Lagoon. But what could you do, Marnie wondered, when it was true love? Christabel kept some sparkly crystal tears in a bowl, and *everyone* knew you only cried crystal tears when it was true love.

Marnie thought about the wish she had recently made for her aunt's happiness. Queen Maretta herself had magically appeared and granted the wish. Perhaps right now, Christabel and Arthur were secretly getting married!

'Horace?' said Daphne, waking Marnie from her daydream. 'Light.'

The large angler fish above the kitchen table switched on his light. The rocky cave filled with a cosy gleam.

'So!' said Daphne. 'Queen Maretta's Palace! I went there on a school trip when I was your age too. It is the most beautiful building in the whole lagoon.' She took a large scoop of algae curry and put it in her mouth. She chewed and swallowed, screwing up her face. 'Yum,' she said, a little fiercely.

The palace was a long way away. Marnie hoped she wouldn't be sick on the journey. She certainly *would* be sick if she ate her dinner.

'I want to see the Jewel Room, with the famous Ocean Orb of Truth,' she said aloud as she pushed her curry around her plate. 'Queen Maretta used it to see the truth about the war with the storm sprites — that storms were good for the lagoon's ecology — and saved the merfolk from any more battles! Though I'm not sure I'd be brave enough to look in the Orb. Apparently it shows you the truth about every naughty thing you've ever done as well. Can I please take some sand dollars for the giftshop?'

The door to the cave burst open. Christabel Blue, star of the *Big Blue Show* and the most famous mermaid in Mermaid Lagoon, swam inside.

'Sorry I'm late,' Christabel said. Horace's light reflected off her huge crystal necklace and bounced little swirls of brightness off the rocky walls. 'The traffic was terrible. Have you ever tried swimming through a school of tunafish?' She frowned and sniffed. 'What *is* that terrible smell?'

She took off her sea-moss coat and hung it on a barnacle hook by the door. Then she unclipped Garbo's lead. Garbo shot into a corner and did a big wee. Marnie giggled.

'I wish you would train that naughty little fish to do her business outside, Chrissie,' said Daphne. 'We're having dinner.'

'You didn't answer my question,' said Christabel.

She gave Marnie a big lipsticky kiss on the top of her head. 'It smells like King Neptune's armpits in here.'

'It's algae and sand curry,' Marnie explained.

'*Pooh!*' said Christabel. 'Let's send out for a takeaway. I know a charming octopus who does marvellous things with seaweed noodles. I'll send him a scallop right away.'

She dug around in her pearl-studded handbag and pulled out a dainty little scallop. Tucking a note into the scallop's beautiful fan-shaped shell, Christabel opened the door again and sent the scallop on its way.

Daphne defiantly ate more of the green sludge. 'It's delicious,' she said. 'And extremely good for you.'

As her aunt settled down at the table, Marnie thought she looked a bit distracted. She darted little glances at Christabel over her broken driftwood fork.

'Where have you been, Aunt Christabel?' she asked at last, as Daphne scraped up the last fronds of algae from her plate.

'Here and there,' said Christabel vaguely. 'What are you up to tomorrow, darlings?'

'We're going to Queen Maretta's Palace,' Marnie explained. 'Everyone says it's got an *amazing* giftshop.'

'But we're not going for the giftshop,' said Daphne. She took another brave bite of curry. 'We're going for the history! The architecture! The experience!'

'Do you remember our school trip there, Daffy?' Christabel asked. 'We had a lot of fun in the air fountain. If you put your mouth on an air jet,' she told Marnie, 'you can do the most amazing burps.'

Daphne sighed. 'Honestly Christabel, you are *terrible*.'

'What can I say?' said Christabel. She gave a faint smile. 'I live life to the full.'

7

'Why don't you come as well, Aunt Christabel?' Marnie asked.

Christabel waved a hand. Her rings glittered in Horace's light. 'School trips aren't really my thing, darling,' she said. 'Ah, here is the octopus with our noodles already. Didn't I tell you he was *marvellous*?'

Chapter Two

Marnie woke up with a flip-flopping feeling of excitement, as if there was a fish in her tummy trying to get out. Today was the day she would see Queen Maretta's Palace with its gleaming crystal windows and famous coral gardens and brilliant giftshop! She hurried to the bathroom to wash her face and scrub her tail with a sea sponge until it gleamed. Then she put on her school jumper, brushed her hair fifty times – she was too excited to do the full one hundred strokes – tied it up with a pearl bobble and swam into the kitchen.

Everything was dark.

'Mum?' Marnie said, peering around in the gloom. 'Horace?'

Horace floated sleepily out of his hole in the ceiling and switched on his light. Marnie gazed at the empty breakfast table.

'Mum!' she shouted. 'We're going to be late!'

A terrible groaning sound came from Daphne's bedroom. Marnie swam down the corridor. Horace followed with his swinging light.

'Is everything all right?' Marnie asked, putting her head around her mum's door.

Daphne was lying in bed. Her face was the same colour as last night's curry. 'Not . . . feeling well,' she croaked.

Panic gripped Marnie. 'But we've got the school trip,' she said.

Daphne groaned again. There was a nasty farty

sound, followed by an ill sort of smell. A cluster of greenish bubbles rose to the rocky ceiling of the cave. 'I'm sorry, darling,' she gasped. 'But I really don't think . . . Urgh . . .'

Christabel appeared at Daphne's bedroom door, yawning and patting her hair.

'Aunt Christabel, what's the matter with Mum?' said Marnie.

'Algae and sand curry,' said Christabel, wrinkling her nose. 'Daffy, you poor thing. I always said that health food was bad for you.'

'I feel dreadful,' said Daphne.

'You smell dreadful too,' said Christabel. 'Let's open a window. A few squirts of perfume wouldn't go amiss either.'

Marnie felt anxious. 'But . . . what about my trip?' she said.

Daphne propped herself up in bed. Her eyes were bloodshot and bleary. 'I'm so sorry, Marnie,' she said. 'But I can't possibly come.'

'*You* didn't eat the stuff, darling,' Christabel said, putting a comforting arm around Marnie's shoulders. 'You can still go to the palace.'

Tears sprang to Marnie's eyes. 'But it was going to be really fun with Mum,' she said. 'And we were . . . we were going to go together . . . '

'There, there,' said Christabel as Marnie burst into tears. 'Perhaps I could come instead? I know I'm not your mother, but I can be quite fun sometimes. And I find myself . . . a little freer these days.'

Marnie wiped her eyes. 'But you said school trips weren't your thing.'

'But my niece very much IS my thing,' said Christabel. 'And we can't have you in tears. Crying blotches the skin.'

Marnie felt better. She threw her arms around her aunt's tummy. 'Thank you!'

she said. 'But are you sure you won't be missing something important? You have your radio show and all your work.'

Daphne farted again, extremely loudly. Horace backed out of the room.

'What can be more important than escaping this terrible pong?' said Christabel. 'I'll send a scallop to the studio and postpone today's recording. Daffy darling, will you be OK by yourself?'

Daphne waved a hand weakly. 'I'll be fine,' she said. 'Take some sand dollars from the clam in the kitchen for the giftshop, Marnie. Don't forget to appreciate the architecture . . . urgh . . .'

Christabel gently shut Daphne's door. 'I'd better get ready then, hadn't I?' she said.

Marnie glanced at the starfish clock in the kitchen. 'We're supposed to be at school at quarter past the morning starfish,' she said. 'It's already quarter to.'

Christabel swam back to her bedroom. 'Plenty of time,' she said. 'Go and have some breakfast. I'll be out in a tick.'

Marnie helped herself to a bowl of Coral Crunch. She brushed her teeth. She took her packed lunch out of the cold-cave box — three seaweed wraps, a bottle of algae juice and a packet of sea-cucumber slices — and slid it into her lunchbox. She tickled the kitchen clam so it opened its shell and let her take out two sand dollars. She carried a warm drink to her mum and kissed her goodbye. Then she sat down on a stool and waited for her aunt.

As the starfish clock arms moved to the top, Christabel swam out of her room. She looked exactly the same as when she had swum INTO her room.

'Aren't you dressed yet?' Marnie said.

'I have everything under control,' said Christabel. 'Have you seen my sea-mud face cream?'

'But Aunt Christabel . . .' Marnie began.

Christabel swam into the bathroom and shut the door. Marnie tidied the kitchen to take her mind off the time. Perhaps she ought to go without her aunt. It really was getting very late. Lady Sealia was very funny about punctuality.

Christabel sailed out of the bathroom as the starfish clock arms edged towards five past. Her hair and make-up were perfect, but she was still in her sea-moss dressing gown. 'Just one or two more things,' she said.

'Like clothes?' said Marnie.

Christabel wagged her finger. 'I just need a teensy bit more time to find my favourite sea-silk jacket.'

'They're going to leave without us!' Marnie shouted as Christabel vanished back into her bedroom.

'It's so important to present a stylish face to my fans,' Christabel shouted back. 'I can't go out looking anything but my best.'

At ten past the starfish, Christabel drifted back into the hall, patted her hair in the hallway crystal mirror, attached an enormous pair of coral earrings, clipped Garbo on to her lead, scooped up her pearl-studded handbag and struck a pose.

'How do I look?' she said.

'You look **VERY LATE INDEED**,' Marnie said crossly.

'I'll just send a quick scallop to the radio station,' said Christabel, hunting through her bag.

'Can you do that on the way?' Marnie pleaded.

The lagoon was busy with early-morning traffic. A shoal of groupers were causing a bottleneck, and the water was thick with impatient tails. Messenger scallops flashed through the glittering water. Marnie dodged through the crowds, dragging Christabel with her.

'It's Christabel Blue!' squealed a dark-haired merman with three tigerfish on matching leads. 'Christabel, I *adore* you. Can I have your autograph?'

'Well of course . . .' Christabel began.

'Sorry,' said Marnie firmly, seizing her aunt's hand. 'Not today.'

School Rock finally came into view. Marnie swam hard, pulling Christabel with her. She could see the whole of her class floating around a huge whale shark near the main entrance to the school.

An octopus in glasses was frowning in her direction.

'Late, Marnie Blue!' Miss Tinkle said. 'Typical!'

Chapter
Three

'Sorry, Miss Tinkle!' Marnie panted, clutching her side. 'We swam as fast as we could.'

There was a rush of excited chatter among the first years as they recognised Marnie's aunt.

'Christabel!' squeaked Mabel Anemone. 'You're my favourite singer in the whole ocean!'

Marnie rolled her eyes. It was so *weird*, how everyone went crazy over Christabel all the time.

Miss Tinkle folded her eight arms four times across her chest. She looked suspiciously at Christabel. 'I thought your mother was joining us, Marnie?' she said. The octopus was **NOT** a Christabel Blue fan.

There was a glint in Christabel's eye. She didn't like Miss Tinkle much either. 'Daffy has a bad case of the bubblers, Miss Tinkle,' she said. 'I've come instead.'

Miss Tinkle looked confused. 'The bubblers?'

'Brown thunder,' explained Christabel sweetly. 'Booty belches. Bottom blasts.'

Miss Tinkle looked horrified. The first years burst out laughing. Gilly whispered something in Mabel's ear, then waved her hand in front of her nose, smirking.

Marnie blushed bright red. It wasn't difficult to guess what Gilly was whispering about. Marnie's best friends Pearl and Orla smiled at her sympathetically.

Mr Scampi the oceanography teacher and Lady Sealia herself were also joining the trip. Lady Sealia sat in the front seat of her seashell carriage with her dogfish Dilys asleep on the seat beside her, tapping her fingers on the carriage windowsill. Typhoon the seahorse snorted and grumbled in the carriage harness. Mr Scampi clacked his lobster claws together and bowed to Christabel.

'Always a delight, Miss Blue,' he said, twirling his moustache.

'You **ARE** a darling,' said Christabel. She glanced at the whale shark. 'Are we really travelling on this clapped-out old thing?'

The school whale shark was old and a bit deaf. His chin was resting on the lagoon bed and he was snoring gently, making the water ripple.

'Yes,' snapped Miss Tinkle. 'He seats twenty-nine very comfortably.'

'The seashell carriage would be better,' said Christabel, waving at Lady Sealia's carriage. 'I gave up public transport years ago.'

Gilly whispered something else to Mabel. Marnie

stared at her tail, feeling awkward. It was easy to forget how diva-ish her aunt could be sometimes.

'We shall be in six groups of five: four students and one adult,' Miss Tinkle said. 'Please listen for your names and join the adult in charge of your group. You must stay with your group AT ALL TIMES. We cannot lose anyone. Ellie Plankton, Hali Fysshe-Fynne, Kerri Kelp-Matthews and Salmonella Stone – you will be with Mr Kelp-Matthews.'

Kerri Kelp-Matthews' dad was a cheery looking merman with an explosive orange beard. He had come as one of the parent volunteers. His group clustered around him.

'Mabel Anemone, Marnie Blue, Pearl Cockle and Orla Finnegan will be with Miss Blue,' Miss Tinkle continued.

Marnie beamed as Pearl and Orla swam over. The trip wouldn't be the same if she wasn't with her two best friends. Mabel gave a squeal of excitement and started swimming towards Christabel too.

Gilly grabbed Mabel's arm. 'Mabel's going to be in *my* group, Miss Tinkle,' she said. 'Aren't you, Mabel?'

Mabel looked unhappy, but stayed where she was.

'Lupita Barracuda, Allira Bladder, Treasure Jones and Mintie Spratt will be with me,' Miss Tinkle went on.

23

Gilly tossed her curly blonde hair. 'Miss Tinkle! Make sure I'm with MABEL.'

Miss Tinkle ignored Gilly. 'Dora Agua, Fresca Brooke, Ripley van der Zee and Kenda Wells, you will be with Mr Scampi. Nerida Attwater, Salina Fysshe-Fynne, Cordelia Glitter and Gilly Seaflower will be supervised by Lady Sealia.'

Lady Sealia gave a queenly wave from the carriage. Typhoon snorted in his harness and kicked hard with his bony tail. No one dared to ride or even *pat* Typhoon, but he made an excellent carriage seahorse when he was in the right mood. Which wasn't often.

'I can't wait!' said Pearl, pushing her glasses up her nose. 'Everyone says Queen Maretta's ultra-rare fish collection is off the REEF.'

'Who cares about fish when there's a giftshop?' said Orla. She linked arms with Marnie. 'This is going to be SO cool.'

'And finally,' said Miss Tinkle, 'Jaya Wetson, Finnula Gritt, Marina Bailey and Zarya Sand-Smith will be with Dr Wetson.'

Marnie could hardly see Jaya Wetson's mother

through the swarm of scallops that surrounded her. Several scallops were snapping their shells at Dr Wetson's nose, trying to get her attention. Others were flapping away, clutching important messages in their shells.

'But what about me and Mabel?' insisted Gilly.

Miss Tinkle peered at Gilly over her spectacles. 'Mabel is with Miss Blue and you are with Lady Sealia, Gilly,' she said. 'There will be no changes. We simply don't have time.'

'And we all know whose fault **THAT** is,' said Gilly, with an angry stare at Marnie.

Marnie bit her lip. Gilly was always picking on her.

The first years swam aboard the whale shark and settled down on his spotty back.

Gilly grabbed Mabel's hand.

'Miss Tinkle said I had to stay with my group,' said Mabel hopefully.

'You can sit with me on the whale shark though,' said Gilly.

'The best seats are always at the back. Come on. Before the *losers* get them.' She shot another mean look at Marnie and dragged Mabel down to the whale shark's tail.

Marnie dipped her head and concentrated on fastening her seaweed seatbelt.

Christabel was still lingering beside Lady Sealia's seashell carriage. 'I could squeeze into the carriage with you, Lady Sealia,' she suggested. Garbo teased Typhoon, darting around him. The grumpy seahorse lashed his tail. 'Dilys won't mind sitting on your lap.'

'Come along, Miss Blue,' Miss Tinkle said, tapping several of the starfish watches that she wore on her tentacles. 'All aboard.'

The gleam was back in Christabel's eyes. 'Very well,' she said. 'Goodbye Typhoon, darling. Be good and **FAST** for Lady Sealia, won't you?'

And she gave Typhoon a cheery pat on the neck.

No one touched Typhoon. **NO ONE**. His eyes bulged. His fins bristled. He roared with fury. And then he took off, the seashell carriage bumping and flying along behind him. The sound of Lady Sealia's screams drifted on the current. Then they were gone.

Chapter Four

'Do you think Lady Sealia is there yet?' asked Pearl.

'She probably got there hours ago,' said Orla. 'If Typhoon swam that fast the whole way.'

The whale shark lumbered along the seabed, keeping his mouth wide open for krill. Gilly and Mabel were the only mermaids sitting at the back. They were both looking a bit green as the whale shark swished his tail around.

Most of Marnie's class had already opened their packed lunches. Kelp fritters, seaweed rolls and sea-cucumber slices were swapped. Sea-anemone juice was traded for fizzy whelks and minnow chews. Garbo was swimming up and down, scrounging for snacks. Everyone was telling jokes.

'What do you call a mermaid that swims really fast?' asked Orla. 'A blurmaid!'

'What did the shark say when he ate the clownfish?'

Pearl returned. "'This tastes funny.'"

'What do you call this sandwich?' said Christabel.

'I don't know,' said Marnie with interest. 'What DO you call this sandwich?'

'It's not a joke, darling,' said Christabel. She was holding one of Marnie's sandwiches between two fingers. 'I am curious to know the answer.'

'It's a seaweed wrap,' said Marnie, taking it back. 'It's my favourite.'

'A seaweed wrap is a beauty treatment,' said Christabel. 'Not a sandwich.' Opening her handbag, she pulled out a pretty packet of sugar-kelp cookies and nibbled them.

'I feel sick, Miss Tinkle,' moaned Mabel, still sitting on the whale shark's swishing tail.

'Move then, you silly girl!' said Miss Tinkle.

Mabel swam up the whale shark's back and sat down with Marnie's group. Gilly folded her arms and looked furious.

'Sugar-kelp cookie?' said Christabel, offering Mabel a biscuit.

'Thank you,' whispered Mabel. 'Can you sign it please?'

Christabel looked surprised. 'You want me to sign a biscuit?'

'Maybe I'll just keep it,' Mabel said adoringly. 'With my special things.'

'Waste of a good biscuit,' said Orla, swiping it from Mabel and crunching it up.

Miss Tinkle clapped her tentacles. 'Let's have a sing-song!' she said.

The mermaids groaned.

'How about "Ten Green Shipwrecks"?' suggested the octopus teacher brightly.

'Ten green shipwrecks broken on the rocks,

OH, ten green shipwrecks broken on the rocks . . .'

'I love your music so much, Christabel,' stammered Mabel. 'I'd like to be a singer when I'm older.'

'And I'm sure you'll be marvellous,' said Christabel warmly. 'You have music in your blood.'

'How can you tell?' Mabel said in amazement.

'The signs are all there, darling.' Christabel patted Mabel's hand. 'There is music in your speaking voice.'

Mabel beamed. 'My gran was a singer. I hope one day I'll be just as good as her.'

'Will you sing us a song, Christabel?' asked Dora.

'Yes!' Mabel gasped. 'Sing "Clamshell Heart"!'

'Sing "Wave Goodbye"!'

'Of course I'll sing,' Christabel said. 'How about my latest single, 'It's Cod to Be You'?'

'Ooh!' sighed the mermaids. 'It's Cod to Be You'

had been all over Radio SeaWave for weeks. Everyone knew the words and the catchy tune.

'*And if one green shipwreck is towed back to the docks,*' Miss Tinkle was still singing loudly. '*There'll be EIGHT GREEN SHIPWRECKS BROKEN ON THE ROCKS.* Come along now!'

'*Eight-a green-a sheepwrecks, broken on the rocks,*' sang Mr Scampi dutifully. He had a strong accent when he sang, and was a little flat.

'*It's cod to be you, ooh, ooh, it's cod to be you,*' Christabel sang, in her distinctive husky voice. '*Out here in the sea, just leave it to me, it's cod to be you . . .*'

Everyone swayed to the tune. Mr Scampi stopped singing 'Ten Green Shipwrecks' and waved his lobster claws above his head. Dr Wetson scooped up all the messenger scallops which had followed her from School Rock, tucked them into her clamshell briefcase and joined in.

Still sitting by herself at the back of the whale shark, Gilly looked like a bad-tempered barracuda.

'You're rather good,' Mr Kelp-Matthews told Christabel. 'Have you thought about a singing career?'

Miss Tinkle made it to five green shipwrecks before she gave up. Marnie felt a little sorry for her teacher, until Christabel moved on to the timeless classic, 'In It to Fin It'. Then she forgot about everything except the music.

'I can see it!' Pearl shouted. 'I can see the palace!'

The coral walls and towers and courtyards of Queen Maretta's palace were peeping over the horizon. A thousand crystal windows winked and glittered like underwater moonbeams. An impossible number of glimmering shells decorated the walls. Marnie couldn't believe how colourful it was. It was if a whole rainbow had fallen into the sea.

The mermaids all rushed out of their seats and gathered on the whale shark's nose to stare at the view.

'I read that the whole palace grew out of the seabed one stormy night,' said Hali Fysshe-Fynne.

'That's a load of fishrot,' said Hali's twin sister, Salina. 'It grew out of a pearl that King Neptune dropped.'

'Did not, barnacle brain,' said Hali.

'Did too,' said Salina. 'And YOU'RE the barnacle brain.'

'Back in your seats, everyone!' said Miss Tinkle.

'The official history of the palace is unknown, but we do know that it has been here for over a hundred years. Queen Maretta herself is long gone, of course, although she makes an occasional magical appearance.'

The other mermaids looked at Marnie, who blushed. Everyone knew she'd met the fabled mermaid queen herself, not so long ago.

The whale shark suddenly sneezed from the weight on its nose. Mintie Spratt fell off.

'This trip is brilliant and we haven't even got there yet,' said Mabel happily as they pulled Mintie out of a clump of red weed.

Up close, the palace was even more extraordinary. Marnie stared at the great air fountain, which spurted and bubbled and fizzed, and at all the mermaid tourists gathering in the enormous courtyard in front of the huge coral doors.

'Oh! I forgot my medicine today,' said Pearl anxiously. She was allergic to coral.

A furious Lady Sealia was sitting on the edge of the air fountain. Dilys hung around her neck like a limp eel. Typhoon and the carriage were nowhere to be seen.

'You're late,' Lady Sealia said as the mermaids climbed off the whale shark.

36

'I think maybe you were early, Lady Sealia,' said Christabel.

Lady Sealia fixed Christabel with the sort of look that would melt an iceberg from the bottom up. 'Poor Dilys is feeling *quite* unwell,' she said.

'Perhaps it was something she ate,' Christabel suggested. She swept her sea-moss scarf around her neck and waved at someone behind Lady Sealia. 'Barbela, darling! How marvellous to see you!'

Barbela was one of the palace guards, and one of the largest, strongest mermaids Marnie had ever seen. Her muscles were like rocks. She was wearing a magnificent uniform encrusted with pearls and carrying a very large trident.

'Christabel Blue!' Barbela said. 'An HONOUR to have you at the palace today!'

Merfolk started to gather, drawn by Christabel's star quality. They pressed and pushed, trying to get as close as they could.

'Can I have a shellfie, Christabel?'

'I love your jacket!'

Christabel struck a few poses, waving and smiling. Marnie and her friends were jostled about by the crowd. Someone fell into the air fountain, and was whooshed straight up on a jet of bubbles. It was all a little scary.

'Stand **BACK**,' bellowed Barbela. 'Keep your distance from Miss Blue, please!'

The crowd melted away at the sight of Barbela's trident. A few hung around, staring and whispering. Barbela glared, and soon they drifted off as well.

'What a lot of unnecessary excitement,' said Lady Sealia.

'Thank you Barbela,' Christabel said, straightening her sea-silk jacket. 'You're an angelfish.'

'Always at your service, Miss Blue,' said Barbela.

Miss Tinkle had turned purple with irritation. 'Time for lunch,' she said. 'Unless Miss Blue has other ideas more suitable for *famous mermaids*.'

Christabel put on her sunglasses. 'Now that you mention it, Miss Tinkle,' she said, 'I'm going to take my group for lunch in the palace restaurant. It will be more private there. I'm sure you understand.'

'Cool!' said Pearl eagerly. 'What's on the menu?'

Christabel smiled. 'We'll have samphire soup to start, I think, followed by sea-grapes and arame biscuits,' she said. 'Then shredded sea palm with just a *touch* of pearl extract for dessert. How does that sound?'

Pearl clapped with excitement. Gilly looked like she'd eaten a sea slug.

'Will you sign a sea-grape for me, Christabel?' asked Mabel.

'You are SO weird,' said Orla.

'FINE,' Miss Tinkle said, even though it plainly wasn't fine at all. 'The rest of us will eat our lunch by the air fountain. Then we'll meet straight afterwards in the Great Shell Hall. No dawdling! We have a LOT to get through today!'

Marnie was glad Barbela swam with them through the palace to the restaurant. Word had spread, and there were Christabel fans around every corner and lurking behind every door.

'I love you, Christabel!'

'Christabel's my favourite name!'

Barbela swelled up like a sea-serpent every time someone got too close, and waved her trident.

'It's the price of fame, darlings,' Christabel explained as they sat at a restaurant table beside a huge crystal window with a view over the coral gardens, with Barbela keeping guard. 'Who would like a sea-grape?'

Marnie wasn't hungry. She'd only just eaten her seaweed wraps and sea-cucumber slices. And anyway, the other diners were watching them and it was putting her off. So she just looked around the grand restaurant with its pearl-studded statues and shell chandeliers, and gazed at the pudding trolley with its gleaming dishes of pearl extract. The lobster waiters whisked about, carrying bowls of pretty pale-green samphire soup high above their heads.

'I'm having the **BEST** time with you guys,' said Mabel, helping herself to a cluster of sea-grapes.

'You can hang out with us any time,' said Pearl.

Mabel's eyes widened. 'Really?'

'Sure,' said Orla between mouthfuls of crispy arame biscuit.

'I don't know why Gilly is always horrible about you,' Mabel said. 'You're all really nice.' And then she blushed and sipped her samphire soup.

A lobster waiter scuttled over to their table. 'Miss Blue,' he said with a bow. 'Will you do us the honour of singing?'

'Excuse me, darlings,' Christabel said to Marnie and the others. 'Duty calls.'

She put down her soup spoon, swam towards the huge driftwood piano which stood beneath a crystal dome at the centre of the restaurant, spoke to the squid piano player, and started singing 'Clamshell Heart'.

'You're so lucky to have Christabel as your aunt, Marnie,' sighed Mabel, as Christabel sang and the squid played and the diners applauded.

'Do you think I can have Christabel's soup?' Orla said.

Christabel gave up a lot for her fans, Marnie thought. Even her lunch. She didn't think she'd enjoy being famous.

Marnie and her friends drifted out of the restaurant with Christabel and Barbela and made their way to the Great Shell Hall to join the others.

Everyone was sitting on long coral benches, waiting for them. Mr Kelp-Matthews had fallen asleep. Dr Wetson was surrounded by scallop messengers again. Mr Scampi and Lady Sealia were both staring at a large portrait of a merman king with wild grey hair and an extremely large trident. Dilys floated beside Lady Sealia's head, yawning.

'Good of you to join us,' said Miss Tinkle sarcastically. 'We are now running extremely late. I have held our group tour—'

'How kind!' interrupted Christabel. 'However, we won't need the group tour, Miss Tinkle. I met the most charming merman in the restaurant, who gave us tickets for a VIM – Very Important Mermaid – tour instead. I simply *couldn't* say no.' She blushed a little, and

44

fanned herself with the five gold-edged tickets.

'I'm sure you could,' said Miss Tinkle stiffly. 'If you tried.'

'Saying no to one's fans is always a terrible mistake,' said Christabel. 'Without my fans, I am nothing. I only wish I could have arranged VIM tickets for you all.'

'A VIM tour!' Mabel gasped.

'Does this mean we'll see stuff no one else can?' asked Orla.

'Like Queen Maretta's ultra-rare fish collection?' asked Pearl hopefully.

This was the first Marnie had heard about a VIM tour. Gilly glared at her with fresh dislike. Marnie felt a blush creeping up her whole body, from the tip of her tail to the top of her head.

'So please go ahead without us,' Christabel said. 'And give my *deepest* apologies to the guide for keeping you all waiting.'

Miss Tinkle swelled up like a furious, ink-filled balloon. 'Then we'll see you back at the whale shark at half past the afternoon starfish,' she said. 'And if you are late, we **WON'T WAIT.** You will have to make your own way home.'

'Of course, Miss Tinkle,' said Christabel in a soothing voice.

'Come along then, everyone,' Miss Tinkle said shrilly. 'We don't need VIM tickets! We're all going to have a marvellous time with Colin, who knows **EVERYTHING** about the palace!'

Colin, the group guide, was a sad-looking electric eel in a hat. His tail shot out a couple of sparks as Christabel blew him a kiss. Miss Tinkle made a Typhoon-ish noise, and swept the rest of the group along with her tentacles.

Marnie felt someone barge into her shoulder.

'I bet you're really enjoying this,' Gilly hissed. 'Stealing my friend and lording it over everyone else. You think you're so much better than us, don't you?'

'I don't,' Marnie began, but Gilly had already swum away with a flick of her tail.

'You're very quiet, darling,' said Christabel, as they passed through a large set of golden doors into the palace's famous Crystal Ballroom. 'Is everything all right?'

Marnie didn't want to be ungrateful. Christabel had gone to so much trouble for the group, buying them lunch and getting them such a nice tour. They had gone to the front of the long queue and everything. But she still felt weird.

'I'm not used to the high life, I guess,' she said.

Christabel put an arm around Marnie. 'Come along now, don't be sad,' she said. 'It's fun to have this all to ourselves. Look at these chandeliers! They are almost as big as my best earrings.'

Marnie gazed around the glittering Crystal Ballroom

with its famous wall mirrors. Garbo swam from mirror to mirror, admiring herself.

'I heard there's a SUPER-rare goldflake angelfish in the Royal Collection,' said Pearl. 'Is it true?'

Their VIM guide — a handsome blond merman called Herman — scratched his golden beard. 'I don't know about that,' he said. 'But the chandeliers are home to two thousand lampfish, which light the place up for parties.'

'Pooh to boring lampfish,' Pearl said. 'A goldflake angelfish is WAY more interesting. It can find gold anywhere. Isn't that amazing?'

'We should move on, Miss Blue,' said Barbela, who was still guarding them with her trident. 'A large party is approaching.'

'What a shame,' said Christabel with a sigh. 'Lead on, Herman.' She put her arm on Herman's shoulder. 'Goodness, aren't you muscly? Like a lovely muscly mussel.'

Herman the merman grinned. 'Thank you, Miss Blue. I'm a huge fan, by the way.'

Christabel fluttered her eyelashes and laughed.

Marnie was surprised that her aunt was flirting with Herman. She thought about Christabel's human boyfriend Arthur. She didn't know much about love, but she knew that you didn't usually flirt with someone else.

Orla linked arms with Marnie. 'IMAGINE being at a ball in the Crystal Ballroom!' she said, twirling Marnie around. 'The music, and the dancing, and the ballgowns—'

'What's that?' said Barbela suddenly.

'What's what?' said Orla.

Barbela frowned around at the empty ballroom. 'I thought I saw someone,' she said.

The Crystal Ballroom was completely empty.

'You said there's a big party coming,' Mabel offered. 'Maybe one of them is early.'

Barbela frowned around the room one more time. 'Perhaps you're right,' she said.

'On we go then,' said Herman. 'Follow me!'

'I would follow you anywhere, Herman,' purred Christabel.

Chapter Six

Marnie and the rest of the VIM party left the Crystal Ballroom through a small, mirrored door. It was so cunningly tucked among the other mirrors that it was nearly impossible to spot.

'Queen Maretta's secret exit,' Herman said as they all swam through. 'She was always the centre of attention at the balls, and she used to get very tired of it.'

'I know how she feels,' said Christabel.

'She would slip away when no one was looking and visit her Jewel Room,' Herman explained. 'That's where we're going next.'

They swam down a tall corridor with high crystal windows on either side. Through the windows, Marnie glimpsed the fantastical shapes of Queen Maretta's coral gardens, and the brightly coloured fish that darted among the coral branches.

'Green swordtail, red swordtail, orange butterfly fish,' Pearl said, gazing out of the windows as they swam along.

'Why don't we have dinner some time?' Christabel suggested to Herman. 'I think that we have LOTS in common. We both have tails, we're both terribly good swimmers, and you have enough muscles for both of us.'

'I'd like that,' Herman said.

Marnie tugged at her aunt's sleeve. 'Aunt Christabel?'

'Hmm?' said Christabel.

Marnie wasn't sure how to ask. So she jumped straight in. 'What about Arthur?' she said, in her lowest voice. *'Your boyfriend?'*

'Oh, Marnie!' Christabel exclaimed. 'Arthur and I aren't together any more.'

Marnie's mouth fell open. 'But he came to see you at the Clamshell Show!'

'And I sent him away,' said Christabel. 'Remember? Lady Sealia made it very clear that he could never return. And she was right.'

This wasn't what Marnie had expected. 'But what about the crystal tears?' she said, feeling baffled. 'What about your true love?'

Christabel took Marnie's hand. 'Those crystal tears weren't mine, darling. They were Arthur's. I met him at the East Lagoon Rocks yesterday and gave them back to him. That's why I was late for dinner.'

Marnie couldn't believe it. Everything she'd thought was wrong. 'So Arthur loved you, but you didn't love him?' she said.

'Oh, I loved him,' said Christabel with a sigh. 'But I belong in the lagoon, darling. If I lived ashore with Arthur, I'd lose my tail. More importantly, I'd lose my voice. I AM my voice. The water is my element, not the land. That can never change. Arthur understands that now.'

'But I made a wish when I put on the Golden Glory Crown,' Marnie stammered. 'I wished for you to find happiness!'

'And I have!' Christabel said. 'Since ending things with Arthur, a weight has been lifted off my shoulders. I can concentrate on my career, and you and your mum, and all the other things that make life so marvellous. Like Herman and his muscly shoulders.'

Happiness is a slippery fish, and swims where it wants.
That's what Queen Maretta had said when Marnie made
the wish. It looked like the famous mermaid queen
was right.

'Well,' Marnie said at last. 'As long as you're happy.'

'Happier than I've been in *years*, darling,' Christabel
assured her.

Marnie realised she had a lot to learn about love and
happiness. With a sigh, she put away her thoughts of
wedding parties and tidesmaid dresses.

'What's that?' asked Mabel, pointing to a large,
shell-encrusted door on their right.

'The entrance to Queen Maretta's maze,'
Herman said. 'The Queen loved playing
practical jokes on her guests. She would
trick merfolk into entering the maze,
and then swim off. There are
rumours that some of her

more unpleasant guests never came out again. There's a door at the far end that leads into the Jewel Room, if you know how to find it.'

'Cool!' said Mabel. 'Can we go in?'

Herman shook his head regretfully. 'It's closed for maintenance.'

Marnie felt another rush of disappointment. She'd been longing to see the maze.

'But this is a VIM tour,' said Orla. 'I thought we could go anywhere?'

'Not the maze,' said Herman. 'It's not safe for anyone, even VIMs. But don't worry! We are going to have an exclusive experience in the Jewel Room that you'll always treasure.'

They swam down a long twisting corridor full of bored anglerfish, who switched on their lights as they passed and switched them off again as they left. Herman told them about the portraits on the walls of long-dead royal merfolk and family seahorses. Marnie felt as if they were swimming in a vast circle.

Finally they reached the Jewel Room. The room was large and velvety dark, and the walls glowed with phosphorescent fish. Jewellery lay in tall crystal cabinets all around, sparkling and gleaming.

'Oh!' said Orla, transfixed by the glitter.

Mabel's mouth hung open. Even Pearl looked impressed.

Christabel trailed her fingers over a large crystal display cabinet which held a magnificent golden tiara. 'Exquisite,' she said.

'Try it on,' invited Herman. 'VIM tour guests are allowed to take the jewels out of their cases and play a little dressing-up. Everything is open. Try on whatever you like.' He wagged a finger. 'Just don't steal anything.

We will be checking!'

Marnie, Mabel, Orla and Christabel fell on the display cases with delight. Orla draped herself in crystal and mother-of-pearl. Mabel tried on an opal tiara that nestled in her dark hair like a glowing egg. Christabel hummed as she clipped on a pair of glittering gold earrings. Garbo, who adored sparkly things, was so overcome that she spun around in the fastest circles Marnie had ever seen, causing tiny whirlpools above their heads.

'Aren't you going to try anything on, Pearl?' said Marnie, wrapping a beautiful gold and crystal bracelet around her wrist.

'I'd rather see a goldflake angelfish,' Pearl admitted. She pressed her hand against a display cabinet full of gold rings. 'It would love it in here.'

'I am the Queen,' said Orla, propping up the huge tiara on her head. She held up a giant crystal orb which glowed and shimmered. 'Bow before me.'

'That's the Ocean Orb of Truth,' said Herman. 'It shows the truth to anyone who looks into its crystal depths. But beware! If you've done anything naughty, the Orb will know.'

Marnie gasped. The actual *Ocean Orb of Truth* was in Orla's hands! Queen Maretta had used the Orb to find out the truth about all sorts of things — from naughty courtiers telling fibs to peace treaties that weren't going to be peaceful after all. Orla put the Orb down a little nervously.

'Time to put everything back anyway,' said Herman, checking his neat starfish watch. 'We still have the Royal Bedchamber, the Frozen Bathchamber and the Sparkly Stables to see. The guards will lock up for us.'

They reluctantly put the jewels back in the cases. Christabel made Garbo open her mouth and spit out a pair of crystal rings. Marnie gazed one last time at the Orb, glowing like a great eye on its sea-moss cushion, and followed the others.

There was a sudden crash outside the doors. The guards rushed past Marnie and the others with their tridents raised. Everyone gazed in surprise at a jagged hole in the corridor window. A butterfly fish swam in for a sniff, and then swam out again.

'Vandals,' said Barbela with a sigh. 'Throwing rocks and breaking windows so they can swim inside free of charge. Check it out, you two,' she told the two Jewel Room guards. 'We can't allow anyone into the palace without a ticket.'

Marnie frowned. There wasn't any broken crystal on the corridor's sea-moss carpet. And if someone had thrown a rock from outside, then where was the rock?

A slight movement near the doors of the unguarded Jewel Room caught her eye. But when she looked, there was nobody there.

Chapter Seven

Marnie's tail was weary when they finally reached the giftshop but she soon forgot it. There were model air fountains that blew real bubbles, seagrass notebooks stamped with Queen Maretta's initials, clam rubbers, seahorse pencils, sea-silk scarves, crystal necklaces, Queen Maretta dolls and driftwood rulers studded with tiny crystals.

There was no sign of the others. They must have already visited the shop. It was getting late, Marnie realised. The whale shark was due to leave soon.

'This is always the best bit,' said Orla happily, picking up a pen with a fluffy sea anemone on the end. 'Although the Frozen Bathchamber was cool. That massive ice-block bath! Can you believe it never melts?'

SEAGRASS
NOTEBOOKS
$4.50

'I liked the Sparkly Stables best,' said Mabel. She stroked a toy seahorse which lit up when you pressed its back.

'Do you sell model goldflake angelfish?' Pearl asked the merman behind the till, but he shook his head.

'Gifts for my group,' Christabel said. 'Anything you like, my darlings.'

Mabel picked up the toy seahorse and a large bag of fizzy whelks. 'Even these?' she said hopefully.

'Even those,' said Christabel.

Mabel squealed and swam around in circles, like Garbo in the Jewel Room.

Orla picked up a polished black crystal and clutched it to her heart. 'Thank you, Christabel,' she said, beaming. 'This whole day has been off the *reef*.'

Marnie decided to spend her own sand dollars on a clam rubber. She swam over to the till. To her surprise, she caught a glimpse of golden hair whisking behind one of the shelves.

'Gilly?' she said. 'What are you doing here?'

Gilly Seaflower swam sulkily into view, clutching her pearl backpack tightly to her chest. 'I'm allowed, same as you,' she said. 'You're not the boss, Marnie Blue.'

'Have the others been to the giftshop already?' Marnie asked.

'How should I know?'

'You were with everyone else,' pointed out Marnie. 'Weren't you?'

Gilly pouted. 'I wasn't going to let you steal my best friend and do loads of cool VIM stuff without me,' she said. 'I've been following you **ALL DAY** and no one even noticed.

63

I would be an amazing catfish burglar,' she added, a little thoughtfully.

Marnie suddenly understood. Those times on their tour when she'd thought someone else was nearby . . . It had been Gilly!

'What are you doing here, Gilly?' Orla demanded, swimming over. Mabel followed.

'I wanted to be with Mabel and Mabel wanted to be with me,' Gilly said loudly. 'We do EVERYTHING together. Don't we Mabel?'

Mabel looked uncomfortable. 'You're supposed to be with Lady Sealia,' she said. 'She'll be worried if you aren't in her group.'

'Pooh to Lady Sealia,' said Gilly. She tried to link arms with Mabel.

'Don't do that,' said Mabel. She pulled her arm away. 'You ALWAYS do that. I've had a really nice time today and now you're spoiling it. You can't do what you want all the time.'

Marnie couldn't believe her ears. Mabel *never* stood up to Gilly.

Gilly's mouth fell open. 'But you're my *friend*,' she said furiously.

Mabel lifted her chin. 'I can have other friends as well as you.'

'We like you, Mabel,' said Orla. 'Even if you are a bit weird about signing biscuits.'

Gilly's chin trembled.

'Come on,' said Mabel. 'You can buy something from the giftshop and we can go and find Lady Sealia together. She won't mind when we explain what happened.'

Gilly's eyes filled with angry tears. 'I don't need anything from this stupid giftshop,' she said. 'I've got something a **MILLION** times better.' And she stormed off, past a very surprised Barbela in the shop doorway.

'Do you think we should follow her?' said Marnie.

Mabel looked worried. 'Maybe,' she said.

'No way, stingray,' said Orla. 'Gilly is a pain in the tail. Why are you even friends with her, Mabel?'

Mabel shrugged. 'We like the same stuff. Singing and performing. Gilly understands how important music is to me.' She blushed. 'Your aunt is the same, Marnie. That's why I love her so much.'

Pearl swam over, clutching a little fish necklace. 'They didn't have a model goldflake angelfish so Christabel got me this instead.' She glanced at the shop doorway. 'Was that Gilly? I thought she was in Lady Sealia's group.'

Miss Tinkle's face loomed in the giftshop window. She was pointing furiously at all the watches on her tentacles.

'I think Miss Tinkle wants us to leave,' said Christabel. She waved at the octopus. 'We'll be out in a moment, Miss Tinkle! Marnie, let's buy this scarf to cheer up your poor sick mother.' And she showed Marnie a beautiful sea-silk scarf decorated with tiny seahorses.

After paying for their gifts, they swam out of the shop. The others were gathered by the air fountain, with the whale shark parked and ready to go. Lady Sealia's seashell carriage looked a little dented.

Typhoon floated patiently in the harness. It looked like the morning's ride had tired him out.

'I have bought you ALL a little something,' Christabel announced, sailing up to the whale shark with her scarf streaming behind her. 'To show you how sorry I am that I couldn't get VIM tickets for everyone. You are *all* VIMs in my eyes.' And she produced an enormous bag of fizzy whelks.

There was a cheer. Marnie was suddenly surrounded by her friends, all munching fizzy whelks and asking how the VIM tour had gone. She told them about the Jewel Room and the Sparkly Stables, but left out the bit about trying on the jewellery. She didn't want to sound like she was showing off.

'We had a good time too,' said Lupita. 'Allira stole Colin the tourguide's hat and hid it in a chandelier. Fresca and Ripley pretended to be statues so Mr Scampi thought he'd lost them.'

'Dr Wetson had to resuscitate Salmonella after she swallowed too much air on the air fountain,' Dora added. 'The burp Salmonella did was AMAZING.'

Lupita giggled. 'And Mr Kelp-Matthews kept saying "That Christine Blue girl should be on the radio, she's awfully good."'

'Has anyone seen Gilly?' Marnie asked, looking around.

Cordelia Glitter's cheeks bulged with fizzy whelks. 'Haven't seen Gilly all day,' she mumbled. 'She was supposed to be in our group, but Dilys was sick in the Coral Throne Room and Lady Sealia forgot to do a tail count.'

There was a stir and a ripple in the water. Marnie

saw twenty guards pouring out of the palace doors. Barbela was at the front.

'Can we help you?' said Lady Sealia, peering out of the seashell-carriage window as they were surrounded by shining tridents.

'I'm very sorry about this,' said Barbela. 'But it seems that the Ocean Orb of Truth has gone missing.'

Marnie's eyes widened. The Orb was *missing*? But they'd seen it on its cushion in the Jewel Room.

Barbela pointed her trident straight at Christabel.

'Miss Blue?' she said. 'I would like you and your group to turn out your bags.'

Chapter Eight

'Barbela, darling,' said Christabel in astonishment. 'What is this about?'

'You and your party were the only VIM tour in the palace today,' said Barbela. She kept her trident pointing at Christabel. 'The jewels were unlocked for you to try on. When the guards came to lock up again, the Orb was missing.'

'That's got nothing to do with us,' said Pearl. Her eyes were round and alarmed behind her glasses. 'We're not thieves.'

'I'm sorry, Miss, but facts are facts,' Barbela said. 'Turn out your bags please.'

Lupita looked at Marnie. 'You never said you actually tried the jewels on,' she said.

'A guilty conscience perhaps,' said Barbela, eyeing Marnie.

Marnie felt flustered. 'We put them back!' she said. 'Honestly, we did.'

'A likely story,' snorted Barbela. 'Bags, please!'

Marnie, Orla, Pearl and Mabel floated together, pink with embarrassment as the palace guards tipped their bags out on the seabed and sifted through seaweed hankies, hair bobbles and half-empty sea anemone juice bottles. Marnie's clam rubber bounced away into a clump of seaweed.

'Your bag too please, Miss Blue,' said Barbela.

'Be careful,' Christabel said, passing Barbela her handbag. 'It's by Valentuna.'

'I'm sorry officers, but will this take much longer?' said Lady Sealia. 'We have a long swim home, and Dilys needs her din-dins.'

'The Orb is one of our most important artefacts, Madam,' said Barbela, handing back Christabel's bag.

'We must make every effort to find it. I'm going to have to take Miss Blue and her group for questioning. Follow me.'

'But we are on a schedule—' began Miss Tinkle.

'So are we, Miss,' said Barbela.

Marnie and the others were herded back to the palace like a school of fish.

'Unbelievable,' said Orla furiously as they were jostled along. 'They can't do this!'

'They're guards with tridents,' said Pearl. 'They can do anything they want.'

Marnie's brain was whirling. She was *sure* the Orb had been on its sea-moss cushion when they left the Jewel Room. Who could have—

'Gilly!' she gasped.

Pearl looked around. 'Where?'

'Gilly has the Orb!' Marnie tried to keep her voice to a whisper. 'She was following us ... None of us took it, so it must have been her! When that window smashed, there was no rock or broken crystal inside the palace. Gilly must have thrown something OUT of the window instead, to distract the guards.'

'It worked,' said Pearl. 'I've never seen two mermen swim so fast.'

'Leaving the jewels unguarded!' said Marnie. 'When Gilly said she had something a million times better than the stuff in the giftshop? She was talking about the *Orb*.'

'Is she mad?' said Orla.

'She was just jealous that we did a VIM tour with her friend,' said Marnie. 'It's totally the kind of thing Gilly would do.'

The others had to agree.

'She could go to *jail*!' said Pearl.

Mabel looked anxious. 'I don't want Gilly to go to jail. I know she's annoying, but she's my friend. I should have stayed with her like she wanted. Then none of this would have happened.'

'It's not your fault, Mabel,' said Marnie. She thought hard. 'We have to find Gilly before the guards do.'

'In case you hadn't noticed, we're surrounded by tridents,' Pearl pointed out. 'How are we going to get away?'

They were taken to a cave off the Great Shell Hall. The guards spread out to stop anyone else from leaving or entering the palace. One guard remained outside the cave. One followed them inside.

'I will question you one at a time,' Barbela announced. 'Miss Blue? As the responsible adult, I will start with you.'

'This is all a terrible misunderstanding,' said Christabel. She adjusted her sea-moss scarf. 'But we will all do our best to help. Wait here, darlings,' she said to Marnie and the others.

Marnie, Orla, Pearl and Mabel sat together on a bench as Christabel and Barbela vanished to an inner office. They stared glumly at the guard levelling his trident at them. The guard stared back.

'Atchoo,' Pearl began. 'Atchoo. ATCHOOOO!'

Marnie realised the bench was made of coral.

'What's with the sneezing?' said the guard suspiciously. 'I have a very delicate constitution. I can't be exposed to illness.'

'My friend is allerg—' Orla began.

'ILL,' said Marnie suddenly. She'd had an idea. 'She's really ill. And it's extremely infectious.'

The guard floated back against the cave wall. His trident trembled.

Pearl's eyes were red and puffy now. '**ATCHOOO!**' she said.

'You had better fetch a doctor,' Marnie told the guard. 'My friend is **EXTREMELY SICK**. If she doesn't get some medicine, she will die. So will you,' she added, as an afterthought.

The guard looked horrified. 'If it's so infectious,' he said, 'how come you lot are still alive?'

Marnie stared at her friends. *Help me out!* she wanted to say.

'We were vaccinated just last week,' Mabel said, joining in.

Pearl's face was bright red. Blotches were appearing on her cheeks.

'There, there, Pearl,' said Orla. 'The nice guard is going to fetch a doctor and save your life.'

The guard fumbled for the cave-door handle. 'I'll be back in a minute,' he blurted. 'Stay there.'

The moment he had gone, Marnie jumped up.

'This might be our only chance to find Gilly,' she said. 'We have to swim for it.'

'What about ... **ATCHOO!** ... the guard outside the door?' Pearl asked.

Marnie pointed at another door on the far side of the cave. 'We'll try that one instead.'

They carefully opened the door and peered outside.

'No one there,' Orla said.

With a flash of tails, the four mermaids shot into the corridor.

'Where should we start looking?' said Mabel as they swam along hurriedly. 'The Jewel Room?'

'Why would Gilly go back to the scene of the crime?' Orla said.

'I reckon she got scared when the alarm was raised,' said Pearl. 'She's hiding somewhere, tucked away where the guards won't think of looking.'

'We'll spread out,' Marnie said. 'And search—'

'OI!' said an angry voice.

It was the guard they thought had gone to fetch a doctor. He was floating in the doorway they'd just come through, pointing his trident at them.

'Swim,' Marnie told the others, abandoning any thoughts of a plan. 'Just SWIM!'

The chase began. Marnie led the way, dragging Pearl by the hand. Mabel was fast and soon shot ahead. Orla stayed close to Mabel's tail. Behind them, Marnie could hear shouting and the clanking of tridents.

They had a good head start, but it was hard to keep a sense of direction. Marnie had a feeling the guards knew the twisty palace corridors better than they did. Had they come this way on the VIM tour? She stared at the seahorse portraits and the sleepy angler fish as they sped along, hoping to recognise something.

They tore up crystal tunnels and through big, looming rooms swagged with coral chandeliers that set Pearl sneezing again. The guards were getting closer all the time.

'Gilly!' Marnie called, panting. 'Gilly, where are you?'

'Gilly!' shouted the others. 'Gilly! GILLY!'

A pain was starting to bloom in Marnie's side as they hurtled into a familiar-looking corridor lined with crystal windows. There was a shell-encrusted door set into the wall. Marnie realised they had reached the maze.

'Can you hear someone crying?' said Orla, cocking her head.

Marnie found it difficult to hear anything over the pounding of her own heart. But behind the shell door, someone was definitely sobbing. A funny feeling swept over her: part excitement, part fear. 'Gilly's in the maze,' she said.

'It's like I said,' Pearl pointed out. 'She's tucked herself away. The guards won't go in the maze. It's supposed to be closed.'

'We have to go inside and find her,' said Marnie.

Mabel's eyes widened. 'But we can't go in the maze. It's dangerous. Herman said—'

The shouting and clanking of tridents was closer than ever.

'Herman schmerman,' said Orla. And she pushed open the door.

Chapter Nine

The maze was very dim. Dimmer even than the Jewel Room. The rocky walls loomed in the darkness, and it was hard to see much further than their own hands. Pearl's spectacles gleamed with little sparks of light as a phosphorescent fish swam lazily past their noses.

The sobbing was louder in here.

'Gilly!' Mabel called. 'We've come to find you! It's me, it's Mabel!'

'Mabel?' A fresh burst of weeping echoed towards them. 'Oh Mabel, I'm in so much trouble!'

'We'll help you to put the Orb back,' Marnie said, feeling her way along the wall in the gloom.

'Why did you have to bring Marnie Blue, Mabel?' Gilly complained, sounding more like her normal self. Her voice grew more cautious. 'How do you know about the Orb?'

'It didn't take a brain sturgeon to work it out,' said Orla.

'Orla Finnegan's here as well? I suppose you've got that weirdo Pearl Cockle too.'

'I'm not weird,' said Pearl indignantly.

Orla squinted into the darkness. 'If you're going to be horrible, Gilly, we'll just tell the guards you're in here and they can sort you out.'

'Don't do that!' Gilly sounded frightened. 'Don't leave me. I'm lost and I can't find the way out.'

'Put your hand on the wall and keep turning left?' Mabel suggested.

'I already tried that,' said Gilly with a sniff. 'I just ended up in the same place. I know I'm going round in circles. I keep seeing the same stupid starfish clinging to the wall.'

'What kind of starfish?' Pearl asked with interest.

'Not now, Pearl,' said Marnie. 'We have to get Gilly out.'

'Why aren't there any angler fish in here?'

Orla said in frustration. 'We can't see a thing.'

'My toy seahorse,' said Mabel suddenly. 'It lights up!'

She pressed the button on her toy seahorse's back. The dark water around them began to glow as the seahorse ranged through all the colours of the spectrum: red, orange, yellow, green, blue, purple.

'I feel like I'm at a party,' said Orla. 'Good thinking, Mabel.'

By the changing light of the seahorse, they could see three tunnels in front of them. The tunnels looked like the wide-open mouths of three enormous fish.

'Let's go,' said Marnie.

'How are we going to find our way back?' said Pearl.

'I'll leave a trail of fizzy whelks,' suggested Mabel.

Marnie swam into the first tunnel. The others followed cautiously. Every now and again, Mabel dropped a fizzy whelk on the rocky ground.

'I hope the fish in here don't like sweets,' said Orla.

Marnie hoped the same. But it was the best plan they had.

'Gilly!' she called. 'Can you hear us? Can you swim towards our voices?'

'I . . . don't know. I can try maybe?'

Marnie stopped. A pile of rocks was blocking the way. The ceiling had caved in.

'Herman said the maze was dangerous,' Mabel said,

shivering. 'What if more of the roof falls down while we're in the tunnels? We'll all be trapped.'

It was a nasty thought. Carefully, they swam back to the beginning and chose another tunnel, avoiding the rockfalls and calling Gilly as they went.

'Gilly! GIII-LLL-YYY!'

'I'm running out of whelks,' said Mabel after a while.

Gilly suddenly came hurtling around the corner. She flung herself at Mabel and hugged her tightly in the multi-coloured light.

'You came, Mabel,' she kept saying, over and over again. 'I can't believe you came.'

'We came too, you know,' said Orla.

Gilly let go of Mabel and wiped her eyes. She looked at Marnie, Orla and Pearl. 'Thanks,' she said, a little reluctantly. 'I guess.'

'Now all we have to do is follow the whelks out of here,' said Marnie in triumph.

They all looked at the rocky ground.

'Um,' said Pearl. 'Where are the whelks?'

A tiny fish suddenly whisked past their tails. It was carrying a fizzy whelk in its mouth. They watched with dismay as it shot away through a crevice.

'You know that question about whether fish like sweets?' said Orla. 'I think we just found out the answer.'

They were deep inside Queen Maretta's maze now,

with no way of retracing their route. To make things worse, Mabel's toy seahorse was starting to run out of power. Marnie tried not to panic in the dimming light.

'Any ideas?' she asked the others.

Gilly started crying again.

'On the VIM tour, Herman said there was a second door, that led from the maze straight into the Jewel Room,' said Mabel. 'Maybe we should try and find it?'

'But how?' said Orla.

Pearl made a peculiar noise. For a moment, Marnie thought she was choking on something. 'Goldflake angelfish,' Pearl stuttered. 'Goldflake angelfish coming this way!'

A neat fish with long golden fins had just swum around the corner. It stopped when it saw them. Its dark eyes grew wide. The mermaids stared at it.

'Nobody move,' said Pearl urgently. 'We mustn't frighten it.'

'It's just a fish, Pearl—' began Orla.

'Mabel, do you have any more whelks?' Pearl interrupted. 'Marnie, can I have your hair bobble?'

The goldflake angelfish was still watching them cautiously. Mabel thrust a fizzy whelk into Pearl's hand. Marnie untied her hair and handed over her pearl bobble.

'What are you going to do?' said Gilly with a sniff.

'I'm going to catch it,' said Pearl. She held out the fizzy whelk and the hair bobble.

'I can't believe you're collecting fish right now, Pearl,' said Orla. 'Seriously, there is a time and a place.'

'This fish is going to get us out of here, Orla,' said Pearl. 'Goldflake angelfish can find gold ANYWHERE. This guy is going to find the Jewel Room for us. Come along, little fish. Lovely fizzy whelk.'

Slowly, the goldflake angelfish swam towards the fizzy whelk. As it opened its mouth and prepared to take a bite, Pearl looped Marnie's hair bobble around it and pulled tight. The fish's fins went rigid with fright.

'Hold on to my tail, guys,' Pearl said. 'These little guys swim fast. Especially when they're frightened. **WHOA!**'

The seahorse lights blinked one last time and went out. Marnie got her hand on Pearl's tail just in time. Mabel grabbed Marnie's tail, and Gilly grabbed Mabel's. Orla was the last in the chain, holding on to Gilly with all her might as the goldflake angelfish shot away in the darkness.

The Last Chapter

It was a strange sight: a chain of mermaids all holding tightly on to a small golden fish. They shot up black passageways and down inky tunnels, through curtains of wet seaweed and, once, over a glowing squid with very large tentacles. The goldflake angelfish never paused for a moment.

'Are you sure we're swimming the right way?' shouted Marnie in the darkness.

'Just because it **CAN** find gold,' said Orla, 'doesn't mean that it will find gold **RIGHT NOW.**'

Pearl sounded worried. 'I didn't think of that.'

'I feel sick,' wept Gilly.

They swerved around a tight corner. Orla banged her tail into the wall and muttered something rude. Marnie hoped Herman was right about another door. She hoped Pearl was right about the goldflake angelfish. She hoped a lot of things.

'*Ten goldflake angelfish, swimming really fast,*' sang Pearl bravely.

'*Ten goldflake angelfish, swimming really fast,*' the others sang back. '*And if* ONE *goldflake angelfish . . .*'

' *. . . should find the door at last,*' Marnie sang, gathering her courage.

'*. . . there'll be—* OH!'

Pearl stopped. Marnie, Mabel, Gilly and Orla all bumped into each other's tails.

'OW,' said Gilly.

They were in a large chamber with a chandelier dangling above their heads. Lampfish darted around, throwing spots of light around the walls. Beneath the chandelier was a door with curly crystal handles. It was smaller and neater than the door they'd used to enter the maze. Mabel pushed down on a crystal handle. It was locked.

'Now what?' Gilly wailed.

Set into the wall beside the door was a strange-looking golden dial. The goldflake angelfish sniffed it eagerly.

'Gold,' said Pearl in triumph. 'See?'

Gently pushing the angelfish away, Marnie twisted the dial a couple of times. There was a click and a whir, but the door stayed shut. She ran her fingers over the eight little images set around the dial.

'They're pictures of fish,' she said, frowning.

'Marlin,' said Pearl, pointing to a graceful fish at the top of the dial. She pushed her glasses up her nose and looked a little closer. 'Hammerhead. Angelfish. Ray. Eel—'

'I knew that one,' interrupted Gilly.

'Squid, Barracuda, and Tuna,' Pearl finished.

'It's a puzzle!' said Mabel in excitement. 'I love puzzles. What do they have in common?'

'They're all fish,' said Orla.

'Technically, a squid is a cephalopod,' said Pearl. She was holding the goldflake angelfish again. It sounded like it was purring.

Mabel tapped her finger on her teeth, deep in thought. 'It's probably about the names,' she said. 'What do they all start with?'

'M-H-A-R-E-S-B-T,' said Marnie.

'That's not a word,' said Gilly.

'Say something useful, or don't say anything at all, Gilly,' said Orla.

'Maybe we should mix up the letters?' Pearl said.

R-S-T-E-M-B-H-A.

A-B-E-H-M-R-S-T.

R-T-E-M-S-H-A-B.

Nothing made sense. They spun the dial left, then right. Click, whir. Click, whir. Nothing.

'Maybe it's Maretta,' said Gilly.

'We can't spell Maretta,' said Orla crossly. 'There's only one T and one A!'

Marnie felt a little flicker of hope. 'That doesn't matter,' she said. 'M-A-R-E-T – we've got those letters. No one said we couldn't use the T and the A twice or that we have to use all the letters.'

She twisted the dial carefully. M-A-R-E-T-T-A.

Click, whir . . . CLUNK. Silently, the door opened.

'Neptune's knickers,' said Orla in astonishment. 'Gilly did it!'

Gilly looked more surprised than anyone. They peeped into the familiar, glittering Jewel Room. There were two guards at the far end, beside the main door. They hadn't noticed the second door, or the mermaids peeking around the doorframe. Marnie put her fingers to her lips. She beckoned to Gilly.

'You have to put it back now,' she whispered.

Gilly pouted. 'I don't **WANT** to put it back.'

'Don't be an idiot, Gilly,' said Mabel. 'It doesn't belong to you.'

Gilly took the Orb out of her pearl backpack. She dropped her eyes to the glowing crystal ball in her hands. 'I'm allowed nice things, the same as . . . **OH**!'

She gave a funny gasp. The guards looked round. Marnie pulled the door shut very quickly. For a nasty moment, they all waited for the guards to burst through and arrest them. Nothing happened.

'That was **WAY** too close,' said Pearl.

'Do you **WANT** us to get caught?' Orla hissed.

Gilly had gone very pale. She shoved the Orb at Orla. 'I don't want it now. Take it away.'

Marnie remembered what Herman had said. *The Orb shows the truth to anyone who looks into its crystal depths. But beware! If you've done anything naughty, the Orb will know . . .* She guessed that whatever Gilly had seen, it hadn't been very nice.

'You have to put it back,' she told Gilly gently. 'It's your responsibility.'

'If you don't put it back, Gilly,' said Mabel, 'I won't be your friend any more.'

Gilly's eyes grew very wide. 'OK, I'll do it,' she whispered after a minute. 'But what if I get caught?'

'Do we look like we care?' said Orla, folding her arms.

'We'll distract the guards,' promised Marnie. 'We'll swim out making loads of noise, so the guards chase us. Then you can put the Orb back and swim after us when the coast is clear.'

Gilly held the Orb away from her. She gritted her teeth. Then she nodded at Marnie.

Marnie shoved open the door so that it flew back on its hinges with a **CRASH**.

'Come and get us!' she shouted at the startled guards.

The next few minutes passed in a blur. Marnie, Pearl, Orla and Mabel swam around and about the crystal cabinets, whooping and yelling, beating the water with their tails so that it swirled and shimmered in the glittering, glowing light of the Jewel Room. The guards spun around, bumping into jewel cases and cursing, waving their tridents and trying to work out what was happening. Pearl released the goldflake angelfish, which shot straight at the guards and confused them even further.

'Time to get out of here!' Marnie yelled, hoping Gilly had had time to put the Orb back.

They fled through the Jewel Room door and swam for their lives. Darting and diving, rolling and twisting, shooting high up towards the ceilings and low down so that their bellies grazed the sea-moss palace carpets. The beaded bed-hangings in the Royal Bedchamber tinkled as they passed. They plunged into the chill of the Frozen Bathchamber and dashed through the Sparkly Stables, making the seahorses snort and buck in surprise. Until finally — FINALLY — they made it to the courtyard.

They were free.

Marnie collapsed on the rocky edge of the fountain, clutching her chest. She could hardly breathe. Pearl, Orla and Mabel barrelled after her, almost crashing into the fountain itself. There was no sign of the whale shark or Lady Sealia's seashell carriage. It looked like the others were long gone.

'I did it!' Gilly shouted exultantly, flying out of the Sparkly Stables door a few moments later. 'I put it back! And they already found it. I heard the guards talking about it when I was swimming through the Crystal Ballroom.'

'I think we got away with it,' Marnie said in wonder.

'Thanks to me,' said Gilly with a toss of her long blonde curls. 'I was so quick, you wouldn't believe it. AND I solved the puzzle on the dial.'

'Aaand the old Gilly is back,' said Orla.

'Maybe next time, don't nick any Crown Jewels in

the first place?' Pearl suggested.

Gilly had the grace to blush. Mabel cheered. Orla lay back on the fountain in exhaustion and let the bubbles bounce her around for a bit.

'STOP!'

Marnie gasped as a line of guards swam towards the fountain. Orla jumped up so fast that the bubbles whooshed her almost as high as the palace roof. Marnie glimpsed the wafting sea-moss scarf of her aunt swimming among gleaming tridents.

'You have found the Orb, Barbela darling,' Marnie heard Christabel say. 'Surely that is the end of the matter?'

'This won't take long, Miss Blue.' Marnie could see that Barbela was holding something carefully in her arms. 'Just one tiny look into the Orb and we'll all know what happened, won't we?'

Marnie swallowed. She should have known they wouldn't get away with something as serious as stealing one of the Crown Jewels — even if Gilly *had* put it back.

Gilly hid her face in Mabel's shoulder as the guards surrounded them again. Pearl had turned as white as the pearls around Orla's neck.

Barbela's glance was as sharp as a shark's tooth. The Orb glowed and swirled in her hands. 'What a surprise to find the Orb safe and sound in the Jewel Room,' she said. 'My guards reported a strange disturbance involving four mermaids matching your descriptions. So I'm sure that you won't mind looking into the Orb

for me now? Just to get to the bottom of the mystery.
The Orb knows the truth about
every naughty thing you've done.'
She pointed at Pearl. 'You first.'

Pearl gazed into the glowing
Orb. Her lip trembled. 'I wasn't
going to keep him,' she burst out.
The goldflake angelfish peeped
out from under her school jumper. 'He
followed me and I couldn't make him go away!
Am I in trouble?'

'We're not interested in the fish, Miss,' said Barbela.

Pearl looked amazed. 'But he's part of the Royal
Collection,' she said. 'Isn't he?'

Barbela shook her head. 'There hasn't been a fish
collection in the palace for years. That's a wild one
you've got there. Keep him if you want.'

Pearl sat down on the edge of the fountain,
looking dazed. The angelfish darted happily through
her long red hair.

Orla looked a bit sick as she stared into the
Orb. 'I didn't mean to break it, Sheela!' she said.
Marnie hardly recognised her friend's voice. 'It was
an accident!'

Barbela peered over Orla's shoulder. 'Just a domestic matter,' she told her guards. 'Nothing for us to worry about.'

To Marnie's surprise, Mabel lifted her chin and stared straight at Barbela. 'I stole the Orb,' she said. 'You don't need me to look into it if I'm confessing, do you?'

'If it's all the same to you, Miss, I'd rather know the whole truth. We'll see for ourselves—'

'It wasn't Mabel.'

Everyone looked at Gilly.

'It wasn't Mabel,' Gilly muttered again. 'Mabel is taking the blame for me. It's the nicest thing anyone has ever done for me in my whole entire life.' She swallowed. 'But please don't make me look in the Orb. I already looked once and it . . . it was horrible. I've done loads of naughty things and I saw them ALL.' She clasped her hands together and looked beseechingly at Barbela. 'Are you going to arrest me?'

Barbela leaned her trident against the fountain.

'Taking one of the Crown Jewels is a serious offence, Miss.'

'I know,' Gilly whispered. 'I'm really sorry.'

'She did put it back,' Marnie said. She felt a little relieved that she wouldn't have to look into the strange, swirling Orb.

'That's true, Barbela darling,' said Christabel. 'Let's all be friends now. I'll sign everyone's trident and you can put the Orb back and we can all go home.'

Barbela considered. 'Everyone's trident?' she said. 'Even mine?'

Christabel produced a glittery shell pen from her Valentuna handbag. *To Barbela, the best guard in Mermaid Lagoon*, she wrote in lovely swirls and loops all down the trident handle. *Stay cool! Love Christabel.*

The guards all started chattering.

'Could you sign my trident for my wife, Miss Blue?'

'Could you sign my shirt?'

Christabel signed everyone's tridents and shirts. She signed Herman's muscly arm, with a cheeky little *Send me a scallop!* added at the end.

Barbela smiled goofily at her signed trident. Then she lifted it and pointed it at Gilly. Marnie held her breath.

'You're banned from the palace for life, Miss,' Barbela said. 'Let that be a lesson. Come along now, troops. We have a palace to protect.'

The guards all waved their signed tridents and swam back to the palace. Marnie caught one last glimpse of the glowing Orb in Barbela's arms, and it was gone. The great palace doors swung shut and they were alone in the courtyard again.

Gilly hugged Mabel. Orla hugged Marnie. Pearl hugged her angelfish. Garbo blew bubbles.

'What a day,' said Christabel. She adjusted the sleeves on her jacket and patted her hair. 'I've sent a nice little scallop to fetch us a shark taxi. Shark taxis are the fastest in the lagoon, and so elegant. We'll be home before you know it. Although I would advise you to keep your tails out of reach. It should be here shortly.'

She grinned and paddled her long painted fingernails in the bubbling air fountain.

'Now,' she said. 'Who wants a burping contest?'

Fin

What is Your Mermaid Name?

Find the month of your birthday and your favourite colour to reveal your o*fish*al mermaid identity!

January	Coral
February	Delta
March	Shelly
April	Hallie
May	Nerissa
June	Andrina
July	Harmony
August	Lorelei
September	Marina
October	Serena
November	Cordelia
December	Melinda

Blue	Seagrass
Green	Kelp
Purple	Triton
Gold	Shore
White	Smallcove
Red	Fairweather
Pink	Waverly
Black	Tidesmith
Yellow	Fishmonger
Turquoise	Waters
Orange	Mangrove
Silver	Sandragon

Quiz Time!

How closely were you reading the story? Test your memory with this fiend*fish* quiz!

Question 1: What is the name of Christabel Blue's pet goldfish?

Question 2: Where is the school trip?

Question 3: What kind of sea creature is Miss Tinkle, the music teacher?

Question 4: Which of these is NOT one of Christabel Blue's songs?
a) Clamshell Heart
b) Ten Green Shipwrecks
c) It's Cod to Be You

Question 5: How does Lady Sealia travel on the school trip?

Question 6: What does Mabel want to be when she grows up?

Question 7: What do the guards carry with them?

Question 8: True or false: Pearl has an allergy to coral.

Question 9: What is the name of the fish that helps the mermaids in the maze?
   a) Silver angelfish
   b) Goldflake angelfish
   c) Cornflake angelfish

Question 10: How does Christabel suggest they get home at the end?

Answers:
1) Garbo 2) Queen Maretta's Palace 3) Octopus 4) b
5) Seashell carriage 6) A singer 7) Tridents
8) True 9) b 10) Shark taxi

Telling Tails

The rest of the first years from Lady Sealia's Mermaid School tour Queen Maretta's Palace. They visit the Crystal Ballroom, Coral Throne Room, Royal Bedchamber, Frozen Bathchamber and Sparkly Stables. Write a story about what happens.

Think about:

 What other rooms could there be in the palace?

What do the other mermaids do when they go on the tour?

Does anything go wrong? (For example maybe someone might get lost or play a trick on a teacher.)

What would they buy in the giftshop?

Read page 68 again where Lupita, Dora and Cordelia explain what they have been doing, to give you some ideas!

Top story writing tips:

- Plan what will happen at the beginning of the story, some exciting action for the middle, and an ending to tie it all together
- Use words like 'First', 'Then', 'Next', 'However' and 'Finally' to move your story along
- Describe things so that readers can imagine what's happening — think about what the characters can see, hear, taste and smell
- Draw some pictures to help tell your story
- Think of a fun title for your story

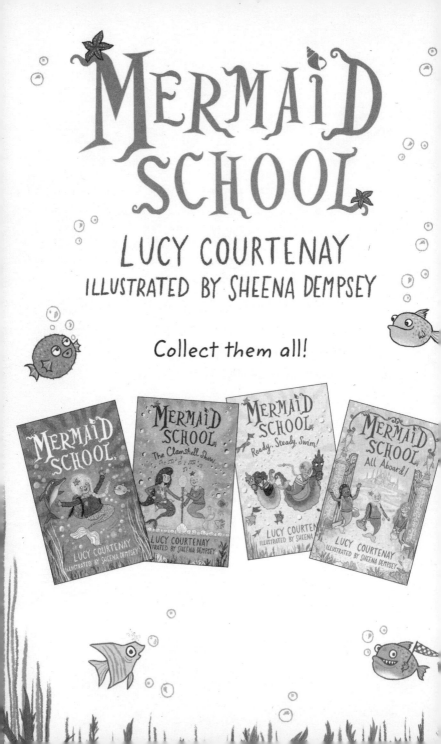